4

Nike's Great Race

Bella Sara™

4

Nike's Great Race

Written by Felicity Brown
Illustrated by Spoops

HarperFestival®
A Division of HarperCollinsPublishers

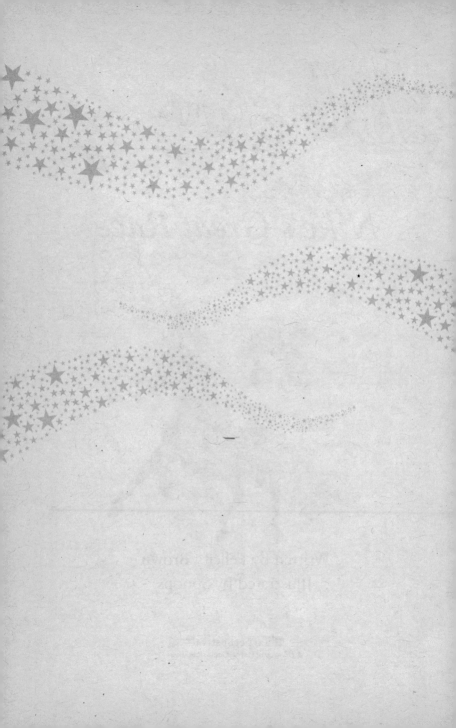

1

"*P*enelope! Come back here!"

As the sun began to rise over Trails End, twelve-year-old Marta Thomas ran after the bovo. The big, blimp-shaped creature ambled along, sometimes running, sometimes hovering just above the ground. Marta caught up to Penelope before the animal floated to the farm down the road. She tethered a rope around the bovo's neck.

"I know you hate being cooped up," Marta told her, "but we can't afford to lose you."

Marta loved Penelope more than all the other bovos, even though Penelope was so much trouble. She couldn't help but admire the bovo's spunk and curious nature, which so often mirrored her own. Often, Marta pretended that Penelope was a flying horse like the ones that soared around the floating island on which Marta and her family lived. Unfortunately, the Thomases couldn't afford to care for a flying horse, so Marta would have to be content with just her daydreams.

As Marta walked the bovo back to the pen, the girl looked out at the other floating islands. She hated that her island was the smallest and poorest among all the Overgaard Skylands in North of North. Although she liked the wide-open spaces of the farmland, Marta couldn't help but be jealous of the majestic homes and neat gardens on the neighboring islands.

Marta grabbed a large pail from

a hook on the side of the fence. She approached a bovo named Lucy and placed the pail under the bovo's udders. Marta pumped the udders, and the pail began to fill up with pink, strawberry-flavored milk. Lucy didn't seem to mind, which made Marta's job easier. She went from bovo to bovo, filling up buckets. She saved Penelope for last, mostly because she was the feistiest.

"Come on now," Marta coaxed. "The sooner we do this, the sooner it will be over."

Reasoning didn't really work with Penelope. But Marta always gave it a shot anyway.

Marta cornered the bovo as she did most mornings and pumped out the milk as quickly as she could. "Thank you, Penelope," she said and looked down at the bucket. It was only half full.

"Penelope, you're going to have to start eating more strawberry clover," Marta told her.

The bovo just grunted in reply.

"I know you prefer peppermint bark," Marta said, thinking of the rich, red-and-white milk that would produce. "But we can't afford to grow it."

Money was already very tight for Marta and her family. She lived with her parents and new baby brother, Toby, in a tiny, damp, one-room house. There was only one window, which made the dark house seem even smaller.

Marta poured the buckets of strawberry milk into two tall cans. Penelope gazed at her with pleading eyes. Marta knew that look.

"We'll go for a walk later," she said. "I promise." She hoisted up the cans and headed back toward the house, happy that her work was done—at least for the morning.

Marta's life had become a lot more complicated in the last few months. Tending the bovos fell to her, because her father was not well enough to do it. While trying to retrieve a bovo that had wandered off the edge of the floating island, Mr. Thomas had slipped and fallen over the edge himself. If a nearby farmer had not heard his cries, her father might never have been found. The farmer had rushed to the edge and seen Mr. Thomas clinging to a rock face with one hand. The farmer had reached down to help, but just as he did so, her father had lost his grip and fell all the way down to the island below! The farmer quickly called for help, and Marta's father was hoisted to safety. But he had broken an arm and a leg, and could not work until they healed.

To make matters worse, the runaway bovo was never found, so there was one fewer bovo. That meant there would be even less strawberry butter and strawberry yogurt to sell at the annual Festival of Lights in two weeks.

It was midsummer, and the sun was already heating up the flat, windblown grasslands. Marta perched on a fence and took a break. She tied her dark brown hair back into a braid. Her looks were nothing out of the ordinary—except for her eyes. They were an exceptional shade of green and could light up her whole face when she was excited.

Marta gazed up to the sky, where beautiful winged horses soared. In their wake, they left contrails of glowing magical essence. That day, the horses and their riders were practicing for the upcoming Trials of Avensgaard—a tournament that dated back hundreds of years. The tournament took place during the Festival of Lights. In it, the riders would perform a series of amazing aerial maneuvers and compete in a dangerous flying race around Trails End. Crowds of people would be coming from far and wide to cheer on the horses and their riders—and hopefully buy some of the Thomases' strawberry yogurt and butter.

Marta sighed as a blue flower

flitter whizzed by to collect nectar from a nearby pink blossom bush. More than anything, Marta wished that she could join the other girls on a flying horse of her own. What she wouldn't give to ride one of the legendary horses her mother used to tell her about when she was little!

Marta had memorized every detail about Bella, Jewel, Fiona, and Thunder. But her favorite of all the legendary horses was Nike, the horse with sparkling wings and eyes that reflected all the colors of the rainbow. Nike was the most beautiful and regal of all the horses of legend, in Marta's opinion. If only someone like her could attract and care for such a noble horse as Nike. . . . But a horse like Nike would no doubt want to live in a grand stable on a huge estate, grazing on the lushest grass and eating the finest oats money could buy. Marta would never be able to afford the things a horse like Nike would expect.

Marta knew she had the determination it took to win the Trials of Avensgaard. She just needed a chance to prove it. She took a moment to picture herself winning the tournament, standing in the winner's circle next to Nike, surrounded by cheering fans. She could see herself winning year after year until she finally retired from the competition and became the legend everyone else tried to live up to. . . .

Marta's daydream was cut short by a high-pitched laugh from above. Tiff Miltondotter, one of Marta's least favorite people, was practicing her moves for the trials on her winged horse, Alrek. The pair flew over a floating hedge.

"Oh, great." Marta groaned. Tiff was the last person she wanted to see today, or any day for that matter. Tiff's family was one of the richest in Trails End—some even said that they were one of the richest in all of North of North. Tiff often liked to remind Marta of this—whether or not it was actually true.

Marta jumped down off the fence and began to walk. She grew angrier and angrier with each step. She picked up a fallen branch and threw it hard across the parched field.

I wish we had more money. I wish we weren't so poor. Why can't I have a flying horse like everyone else?

As Marta looked back over her shoulder at her run-down house and the declining farmland, the fire inside her continued to burn. She wished that caring for the bovos wasn't her responsibility. She wished her father hadn't gotten hurt. *This is so unfair!* she thought, as she watched the girls and their horses swoop overhead. *Why does a snotty girl like Tiff get all the luck? Why can't we be rich, too? Why do I have to work on this stupid farm while they get to play and ride?*

Marta stopped under a big tree and sank to the ground. She thought of the long summer ahead, and tears of frustration began to trickle down her cheeks. *Will it always be like this?* she wondered. *Will nothing ever change?*

fter a few minutes, Marta pulled herself together. Crying wasn't going to change anything. She returned to the gate, where Penelope was mooing loudly.

"Okay," Marta told the bovo. "A promise is a promise. Let's go for a walk."

Penelope's moo went up in pitch, which Marta knew meant that the bovo was excited. Marta removed the rope from Penelope's neck, unlatched the gate, and the bovo ran out.

"Easy, girl!" Marta said with a laugh. She held the gate open for the other bovos to file out. Many of them floated out, as bovos do when they have no food in their stomachs to weigh them down. They all headed toward Strawberry Meadow, a favorite grazing spot for the bovos. It used to be lush and plentiful, but now heat and dry weather had killed off most of the good grazing, and strawberry clover only dotted the meadow.

Marta headed for the trees that sat in a cluster in the center. On a hot day like today, they were great for shade.

When Penelope had filled up on strawberry clover, she let Marta climb onto her back for a while. Astride the bovo, Marta once again fell into a daydream about the Trials of Avensgaard. She pretended that Penelope was the winged horse Nike, and they were flying together in the sky, Nike's magical ribbons trailing behind them.

It wasn't the most convincing of

daydreams. Penelope's large size made her anything but graceful, and Marta sometimes slid right off her wide•back. But it was the closest Marta was going to get to a horse, so she was happy to dream. No one could take that away from her.

Although Tiff Miltondotter certainly did try. If anyone could cast doubts on Marta's dreams, it was Tiff. Now, astride their winged horses, Tiff and her friends landed in an open area in the meadow, kicking up dirt and dust as they landed—right in Marta's path.

Marta shielded her eyes from the dirt, but Penelope got a mouthful. The bovo mooed loudly in distress. Marta leaped off her back and tried to calm the animal down.

"Oops!" Tiff said in a phony voice. She took off her riding helmet and flipped her blond hair over her shoulder. "I didn't realize there was so much dust here. We would have landed somewhere else."

Marta grimaced. She was certain Tiff knew exactly what she was doing, especially when it came to being mean to Marta.

"What were you doing sitting on that filthy creature, anyway?" Tiff asked Marta. She didn't even bother to call it riding.

Marta tried to ignore Tiff's question and kept busy brushing the dirt off Penelope. She really wished Tiff hadn't seen her. How embarrassing!

Tiff and her friends, Britt Jansdotter and Karin Larsdotter, dismounted. All the girls wore riding helmets and breeches. It was their riding jackets, however, that set them apart. On their jacket lapels were very elaborate designs. Each design represented that girl's family's coat of arms. Britt and Tiff's family designs were made up of curlicues and flowers, while Karin's was a more geometric pattern. Tiff, Britt, and Karin were all from families that had long lineages in Trails End, dating all the way back to when Sigga Rolanddotter governed the land. To have such deep roots in Trails End was highly valued. It also made the girls fond of bragging.

Britt removed her helmet and tucked her long, black hair behind her ears. She sauntered up to Marta and Penelope. "Aw, poor Marta. Couldn't afford to attract a winged horse so you have to ride this pathetic bovo instead?"

Marta simply tightened her jaw, but Penelope wasn't as restrained. The bovo nudged Britt backward.

Britt gasped. "Did you see that? That . . . that . . . *thing* almost ran me over!"

Marta knew that Britt was in no danger. Penelope would never actually hurt anyone. But a good scare had certainly been in order. "Good girl," Marta whispered in Penelope's ear.

"I heard that!" Britt fumed as she rubbed at a nonexistent bruise. She retreated to her horse, Roald. The honey-

colored aerial horse snorted his disgust at Penelope.

Roald, Tiff's horse friend, Alrek, and Karin's horse friend, Dagna, were very much like their riders: snobby and proud. Each horse was also fiercely competitive and trained hard for the Trials of Avensgaard.

Even though Marta didn't like their riders, it was hard to hide her awe of the horses. But Marta didn't want the other girls to see her admiration, so she concentrated hard on not staring.

Dagna stamped his forelegs impatiently. Karin patted the horse's brown-and-white spotted flank.

"We'll get back in the air soon," Karin told him. "Can we go now, Tiff? I really need to practice more of my aerial dives."

Dagna whinnied in agreement.

Alrek whinnied, too. But Tiff ignored him. She looked around at the bovos grazing on what little bit of strawberry clover was left in the meadow. "Too bad your bovos can make only strawberry milk," she said to Marta.

Britt agreed. "That's so *common*," she said distastefully.

Marta tried to keep her cool. She didn't want to let the other girls see her upset.

"I guess it's hard when your father falls off an island," Tiff said, making it seem like Mr. Thomas was simply a klutz.

Marta's eyes narrowed. Tiff smiled wickedly, seeing that she'd hit a nerve. "But I might try to run away, too, if I had to look at someone as ugly as you all the time," she added.

Marta had been trying hard to keep cool. But she was so shocked by Tiff's outright nastiness that she blurted out the comeback that leaped to her tongue. "So I guess you must run away from the mirror every morning?"

"I . . . I . . ." Tiff fumed,

momentarily speechless. She turned red with rage. "Come on," she snapped at her friends. "Let's not waste any more time talking to this loser."

Almost instantly, Tiff and Britt were back on their horses and in the air. Marta breathed a sigh of relief that the encounter was over. But her relief didn't last long.

Guided by their riders, Alrek and Roald swooped down low over the meadow. They flapped their wings hard, creating a strong wind and lots of dust. Terrified bovos scattered in every direction, lowing and rolling their eyes. Tiff crowed with pleasure as she and Alrek circled back around.

A frantic Marta ran all over the meadow, trying to keep the scared bovos from bolting. It was no use. The blimplike animals were already scattered far and wide over the floating island. Defeated, Marta stopped running and caught a breath. As she glanced around, she noticed that Karin hadn't joined in. With a sheepish look, Karin put her helmet over her short, red hair. Then she mounted Dagna and flew off, her eyes lowered.

A loud moo made Marta spin around again. Britt and Tiff had cornered Penelope by some rocks. The bovo trembled with fear. Marta ran with all her might to the bovo's side.

"That'll teach you to mess with a Miltondotter!" Tiff yelled down to Marta. Then she motioned to Marta's house. "Enjoy your pathetic little shack while you can. The clock is ticking!"

With a flick of his wings, Alrek rose into the air. Roald followed. Marta stared after Tiff and Britt as they flew into the distance.

The clock is ticking? she thought. *What exactly is that supposed to mean?*

It took the rest of the day for Marta to round up the bovos. The skittish creatures were thoroughly spooked by what had happened with Tiff and Britt. Penelope was especially wound up, and it took Marta a while to calm her down. By the time Marta had secured all the bovos in the pen back home, she was exhausted. With sagging shoulders, she walked through the front door of her house to see an unexpected guest.

"Marta," said her father. "This is Harald Miltondotter, Tiff's father."

Marta stayed silent, her eyes taking in the round, rather large man. She wondered why he was there. Then she noticed her mother was crying.

"Mama, what's wrong?" Marta asked, running to her mother's side.

Before she could answer, Mr. Miltondotter headed for the door. "You have two weeks. That's it," he said to the Thomases.

Marta shut the door after him and then spun around to face her parents. "What did he mean? What's going on?" she demanded.

In his mother's arms, baby Toby began to cry from all the commotion.

"There, there," his mother said, comforting him with soft kisses on his forehead. Then she looked up at Marta and took a deep breath. "Mr. Miltondotter is the landlord of this island, among others. We haven't been able to sell enough yogurt and butter to pay the rent."

"But—but *I've* been milking our bovos every day," protested Marta.

"We know, Marta," said her father. "And we appreciate all you've done. But it's simply not enough. We don't have enough bovos. And the bovos we do have need more food to produce more milk, and the clover fields just aren't what they used to be."

"If we don't come up with the money, we'll be evicted," Mrs. Thomas explained to Marta, bouncing Toby in her arms. "We'll have to leave."

Marta sat down on the edge of her bed. She clutched the soft quilt that her mother had lovingly stitched with images of Nike flying through pink and blue clouds. *This must have been what Tiff had meant earlier,* she thought. Tiff must have known her father was going to pay a visit to her family. Marta even wondered if Tiff put him up to it. It seemed like something she would do.

"But Mr. Miltondotter is so rich,"

Marta said, frustrated. She paced back and forth in the small room. "Why does he care whether or not we pay on time?"

"It doesn't work that way, love," her mother explained. Toby's cries had softened to a quiet gurgle. Marta wished it were that easy to make her own fears go away.

"But—but where will we go?" she asked.

A tear ran down Mrs. Thomas's cheek as she looked at Toby in her lap and Marta across from her. "I don't know, my dear. I just don't know. . . ."

Marta stood up from her bed and looked out the tiny window at the grazing bovos. Inside, she felt her anger swell. She felt frustrated that her father wasn't well enough to work. But, even more, she couldn't believe what Tiff's father was doing to her family.

Mr. Thomas hobbled over to his daughter, using a wooden crutch under his one good arm. He reached out and touched her shoulder.

Marta flinched slightly, and her father immediately pulled his hand back. Marta bit her lip. She hadn't meant to hurt his feelings. But she couldn't bring herself to apologize, either. She was just too angry at everything and everyone.

"I'm going outside," she said quickly, and left.

The cool evening air felt good on Marta's flushed cheeks. A picture rose in her mind—the picture she'd been imagining that afternoon, of herself riding to fame and fortune on Nike. Right now that dream seemed farther away than it ever had before. She kicked the dirt with fury. She felt so trapped.

"Why did this have to happen to me?" she exclaimed, as she strode toward the clover fields. "Why can't we just have money and a flying horse like everyone else?"

When no answer came to her, Marta gradually began to slow down—

and cool down.

I have to stop feeling sorry for myself, she realized. *Mama and Dad are relying on me. I'm all they've got right now.*

She knew she would have to appear brave for her parents, even if she didn't exactly feel that way. It was up to her to save the family from ruin. Now she would just need to figure out how. . . .

"I will do it, somehow," she vowed.

Then, to her delight, a shooting star dipped down toward her through the Auroborus. The brilliant light streaked across the sky.

Marta's father had always told her that a shooting star meant something good was about to happen. And now, although she couldn't explain it, Marta began to feel deep down in her heart that she could change her life.

4

At dawn the following morning, Marta woke with a start. She wasn't sure if she was dreaming or if she had just heard a horse whinny. She tiptoed to the window, careful not to wake her mother or brother. She gasped when she saw a winged horse standing outside. With the intricate gem-studded pattern on her forehead and gossamerlike mane and tail, Marta knew immediately who the majestic creature was.

It was Nike!

Marta rubbed her eyes. *I must*

be dreaming, she thought. She quickly wrapped her quilt around her shoulders and walked out the door. She was standing just footsteps away from the beautiful horse. The dry grass felt scratchy under her bare feet. *If I were dreaming, then I wouldn't be able to feel this itchy grass.* A rush of excitement flooded through her. *Could Nike really be outside my very own house?*

Marta took in the horse's magnificent wings and glowing eyes. She took a step closer to the horse and felt her whole body tingle as if a magnetic force were pulling her forward. She wanted to run right up to Nike, but she sensed it was not the proper thing to do. Instead, she bowed her head slightly. In response, Nike bowed.

Raising her eyes, Marta gazed at the large, chestnut brown horse, taking in all her splendor. The horse began to smooth and groom her wings. Marta was in awe. "Your beauty, your grace," she

said to Nike, "you are the most magnificent horse I've ever seen. Are you really . . . Nike?"

The horse stood proudly, emanating a soft glow.

Marta couldn't believe it. Nike! The real Nike that she had dreamed about every day for as long as she could remember was right here in front of her own house!

Marta watched as Nike turned to look at the Thomas family's house. The horse walked slowly around the tiny wooden cabin, looking inside the window and up at the crumbling roof. She snorted.

According to the stories, Nike was used to much grander surroundings. Marta's cheeks burned as she imagined how Nike must see her one-room house. She was even more embarrassed than she'd felt around Tiff and her snotty friends.

"Nike, I can explain. My family

and I work very hard. It's just that things haven't been going so well lately, and my father had this horrible accident. He can't work and—"

Nike stomped as if to command Marta's attention and stop her from rambling. Marta watched nervously as Nike studied her face. She sensed that the horse could see her strong will to succeed.

Marta suddenly had a strange sensation, like something was tickling her forehead—but on the inside! Her eyes widened as she realized what it was. She had heard that horses could communicate with humans by projecting pictures into their heads, but she had never expected it would happen to her! At first, the image was foggy, but as the tendrils of mist cleared, she saw an image of herself, with a determined look on her face as she brought the bovos to the clover fields to graze. Then she saw another image: her riding Penelope with a dreamy smile.

As she studied the image, Marta understood that Nike was trying to tell her that the horse admired her perseverance in hard times and her desire to succeed even if it meant riding a bovo for practice.

Then Marta received a third image. This one was clearer than the first two. She was riding Nike, and they were going through rings and up and over hedges. Marta could see flags and banners. She suddenly realized the image was of her and Nike competing in the Trials of Avensgaard!

Marta's green eyes widened with excitement. "We're going to compete together?" she asked.

Nike nodded and sent another image to Marta. Out of the fog emerged an image of sparkling golden horseshoes.

Marta knew instantly what that image meant. It was the grand prize for winning the Trials of Avensgaard. And the horseshoes were solid gold.

Nike gestured with her head toward the rundown house. Excitement rushed through Marta. Of course! With enough golden horseshoes, she could pay the rent on her family's home! Why, she could probably even buy it outright!

"This is the most wonderful thing that has ever happened to me!" Marta gasped. She ran inside to wake her parents and tell them the amazing news.

A few moments later, Marta's mother stepped outside, cradling a sleeping Toby in a blanket in her arms. Behind her, Marta's father hobbled out using his crutch. Mr. and Mrs. Thomas gazed at the statuesque creature in front of them, overwhelmed by Nike's beauty. They gently bowed their heads. Nike bowed in return.

"What an honor it is to meet you," Mrs. Thomas told Nike, smoothing her skirt with her free hand. Marta watched her mother's face light up with joy. Her mother used to tell her that being in Nike's presence brings a person good luck. Marta could just imagine that that was what her mother was thinking.

Toby squawked, craving his mother's attention. Nike gave a soft whinny and stepped forward to take a closer look. She bent her head down, and baby Toby looked into the horse's eyes with a mixture of curiosity and joy.

"Look how gentle she is with Toby," Mr. Thomas whispered to Marta. Marta smiled as the morning sun warmed her shoulders. She couldn't believe how her luck had turned in just one day.

"The baby obviously likes you," Mr. Thomas said to Nike.

Nike whinnied, and Toby gurgled with excitement.

"Marta tells us that you've come to compete in the Trials of Avensgaard and that you'd like Marta to compete with you," Mr. Thomas said to Nike. "That is very kind of you. Thank you." He turned back to his daughter. "You will need to train and work very hard. Harder than you ever have before." Mr. Thomas's look was serious.

Nike nodded as if in agreement.

Mrs. Thomas cleared her throat. "No offense to you," she said to Nike, "but I already have one injured member of my family. I don't want another one."

"Mama, I can win. I know I can," Marta insisted, grabbing her mother's hand.

"I think Marta can handle it," Mr. Thomas said to his wife. He looked at his daughter. "My brave Marta."

"Thank you, Dad," Marta said softly with an embarrassed smile. She liked it when her father called her that, even if she wouldn't even admit it out loud.

Marta faced her mother. "Mama, it's our only chance to save our land and our house," she said firmly.

She watched her mother cast a glance toward the rickety house. Her heart beat fast. Mama *had* to let her compete. *Say yes, say yes,* she chanted silently.

After a few moments of silence, Mrs. Thomas finally said, "All right, then, you have my blessing."

"Thank you, Mama!" Marta cried.

As she thought of something, though, her face fell. "Wait a minute," she said. "Everyone trains for months for the trials. How are Nike and I even going to have a shot with only two weeks to train?"

Her father reassured her. "Nike wouldn't have come if she didn't think you stood a chance."

Nike whinnied in agreement. A second later Marta received an image of herself riding Nike through pouring rain. It was followed by an image of them flying through the hoops as the sun rose behind them.

She smiled. "I get it," she told Nike. "You're telling me we'll just have to practice all the time, day and night, good weather or bad."

Nike bobbed her head emphatically.

Marta stood up a bit straighter. "All right, I'm in. We won't stop training until we get every move right." Saying the words out loud made it all seem more real. She was determined to work harder than she ever had before in her life.

"Hold Toby for a moment, would you, Marta?" Mrs. Thomas asked suddenly. She hurried back into the house and returned carrying a battered old helmet covered in faded black velvet.

"Great-grandmother's riding hat?" Marta asked, stunned. Her mother's grandmother had been a famous horsewoman. "But you never even let me try it on when I was little."

"I want you to have it," her mother said, smiling as she held it out to her daughter. Mr. Thomas put his hand on his wife's shoulder.

"Are you sure, Mama?" Marta

asked, as Toby cooed happily in her arms.

"May it bring you courage and success," Mrs. Thomas said.

Marta carefully gave Toby back to her mother. When she placed the hat on her head, it was a perfect fit. She looked at her mother gratefully.

"I'll make you proud."

Mrs. Thomas smiled warmly. "You already have."

Nike whinnied. It was time to go. There was a long day of practicing ahead of them.

Marta turned to leave, and then abruptly stopped. "The bovos! Who will take care of them while I train?" How could she have forgotten?

Mrs. Thomas brushed a stray piece of hair away from Marta's forehead, something Marta hardly let her do anymore. "We'll manage, love. I will do my best to tend to them. Even mischievous Penelope." She winked.

Marta laughed out loud. It felt so good—she couldn't remember the last time she had laughed. But then, everything felt good this morning. This morning, for the first time in a long while, Marta felt hopeful.

5

The next morning when Marta woke up, her entire body felt as if it were on fire. Every muscle in her body ached as she stretched. She groaned as she got dressed for day two of training.

Day one had been incredibly hard, especially because she wasn't used to riding for hour upon hour. But when she pictured herself arriving at the trials on Nike's back, it made all the aches and pains worthwhile.

Mrs. Thomas had just finished preparing a hearty breakfast for Marta as the girl sat down at the small table. She took Marta's porridge off the stove and took a seat in the wooden chair next to her daughter.

"Marta, remember when I used to tell you the stories of Sigga and the grand Festival of Lights?"

Marta nodded, her mouth full of porridge.

"When I was a little girl, my great-grandmother used to tell me the same stories—about how the Festival of Lights was once the biggest party you could ever imagine! This was over a thousand years ago—even before great-grandmother's time, if you can believe it," Mrs. Thomas said. Marta giggled.

"Legend has it that Sigga and the other Valkyries would plan for months for the great feasts and celebrations leading up to the festival. Hundreds of horses would travel from all over North of North to Rolanddotter Castle: winged horses, horses that could create fire, even water horses! And the fireworks . . . it was like nothing in your wildest dreams." Marta's mother smiled wistfully at the images in her head. Then she brushed her hands against her lap and got up to tend to Toby in his cradle in the corner.

"Mama, I know the trials aren't as big as they used to be," Marta said, finishing up her last bite of breakfast. "But this is still the most exciting thing that has ever happened to me."

"Oh, I know, love. I know. I am so happy for you. That wasn't the point of my story. What I meant to say is . . . I've been getting this feeling lately that things are going to change. I believe that perhaps you will get to see the restoration of North of North to its former glory. Maybe even before you're an old lady like me!"

"You'll never be old, Mama," Marta said, as she put her dish in the sink. "See you after sundown!" She waved as she darted out the door.

Nike stood in the shade of a nearby tree, her wings folded at her side. Her whole body emitted a soft pink glow. Marta approached hesitantly to offer the mare a red apple.

Nike looked at it skeptically and then sent an image of Marta shining it with the edge of her shirt. Marta grinned as she did so. Then she watched Nike munch on the apple. Even the way the horse ate was regal.

Nike then sent an image of herself and Marta flying in the sky.

Marta's eyes widened. They had not flown the day before. Truth be told, they had spent the entire day just trying to keep Marta from falling off. All she had ever ridden before was a bovo—and Nike was definitely no bovo!

Walking was easy, and even cantering was okay, but trotting was awfully bouncy. It made Marta's teeth rattle. And galloping—every time Nike broke into a full gallop, Marta promptly fell off.

From the images Nike sent her, Marta knew she was supposed to hang on with her knees and thighs, but it wasn't so easy when you were bouncing around like a jumping bean. Certain horses would let their riders put saddles on them. But Marta suspected that Nike would never allow that. She wouldn't even dare to suggest it.

Marta learned quickly that Nike had certain preferences when it came to other things, as well. After they'd been walking for about twenty minutes, Nike whinnied and shook her head.

Marta realized she was holding on too tightly to Nike's mane. "Sorry!" she said apologetically.

Nike progressed from a walk to a trot. But then she stopped abruptly and sent an image of Marta's foot repeatedly banging into her side.

"Oops! I'm so sorry—I didn't mean to kick you! I won't do it again."

Practice had gone like that all day.

By the end of the day, Marta had fallen off six times, and her thighs felt rubbery and exhausted from gripping so hard.

Now, as she thought about actually leaving the ground, she gulped. "I—I'm not sure I'm ready to fly."

Nike just gazed patiently at her.

"All right," she said, trying to push down her fear. "If you think I can do it, I'll try."

Nike walked over to a mounting block and stood still while Marta climbed aboard. Then the mare unfolded her wings. Marta stifled a gasp. She hadn't thought about what it would be like to ride with those huge wings beating the air on either side. . . .

Nike took a few prancing steps and sprang into the air. She gave a powerful thrust of her wings.

"Ahhh!" Marta cried, as she slid down Nike's tilting back and over her rump. She landed in a convenient haystack with a grunt. "Oof!"

The hay was soft, and Marta wasn't hurt—just embarrassed. Nike alighted next to her and regarded her. She sent no mental pictures, but Marta had a strong suspicion that the mare was laughing at her.

The next time she mounted, Marta was determined to stay on no matter what. Nike sent a reassuring image of the two of them taking off in perfect flight, with Marta's legs firmly clamped on Nike's sides and her gaze aimed straight ahead.

Nike took a running start, flapped her wings, and soared into the air. Soon they were farther off the ground than Marta had ever been before.

"We're doing it, Nike! We're flying!" Marta yelled with delight. They spiraled higher and higher. Marta stared in delight at the landscape spread out before her.

Suddenly, a dark shape swooped down from above. Marta had a blurred impression of something big hurtling straight at her. She ducked. Her hands automatically flew up to protect her head—which meant she was no longer holding onto Nike's mane!

"Whoa!" she yelped, as she slid backward off Nike's back. And then she was plummeting helplessly through the air! Her arms and legs pinwheeled. The ground rushed up to meet her.

"Nike! Help me!" she shouted.

Whoosh! A brown blur shot past, plunging downward even faster than Marta. Then, suddenly, Nike was there below her. The mare fluttered her wings to hover in midair. Marta smacked facefirst into Nike's back and buried her fingers in Nike's mane, shaking with relief.

"You saved me! Thank you," she whispered to Nike.

When she could sit up, she gazed up into the sky above her. There was Tiff Miltondotter, flying on Alrek. For once, her friends weren't with her.

"You could have killed me with that stupid stunt!" Marta yelled, furious.

The expression of worry left Tiff's face, replaced by her more familiar smug look.

"Oh, I'm so sorry!" she said with a fake smile. "I didn't see you there."

Marta leaned forward and whispered in Nike's ear, "Meet the competition. That's Tiff Miltondotter."

Nike snorted, her nostrils flaring.

"I know," Marta said. "She really isn't a nice person."

Nike and Marta flew right up to Tiff and Alrek.

"You know, if this were the trials, you would be disqualified for what you just did," Marta said, still fuming.

Tiff pouted. "I said I was sorry. Anyway, it was just an accident."

Marta rolled her eyes. Then she said to Nike, "Come on. Let's not waste our time talking to her. See you at the trials, Tiff."

Tiff gasped. "*You're* entering the competition?"

Marta smiled. "We certainly are." As casually as she could, she added, "Oh, by the way, have you met Nike?"

As Nike turned to fly away, Marta had the immense satisfaction of seeing Tiff's mouth fall open in total shock.

A's the week progressed, Marta and Nike spent every minute practicing for the trials. Marta had finally learned to balance on Nike as she soared in the air. But mastering the aerial maneuvers was not going so well.

"Whoa!"

"Wait . . . wait . . . *wait!*"

"Yikes!"

Marta couldn't help getting flustered by the hedges, poles, and rings magically floating in the sky. Each competitor needed to jump over or through all of them successfully. Marta had gotten to the point now where she felt reasonably sure of staying on Nike's back, but doing complicated maneuvers was another story. Nervously, she remembered that they would be judged not only on completing the maneuvers, but also on how flawless they made them look. Confidence was a huge factor. Unfortunately, in these particular stunts, confidence was something Marta didn't have.

Again and again, she and Nike tried to jump a giant hedge suspended in the air. Although Nike's wings were powerful enough to propel them over the hedge, she had trouble landing on the other side. It was Marta's job to guide and steer the mare just the right way in order to land the jump perfectly. Marta realized now that part of what made the trials so difficult was that the horse and rider needed to act as a single unit.

The trouble was, each time Nike pushed off to fly over the hedge, Marta would tense up. She would grab onto Nike's mane too tightly, or she would cry out, or she would clench her knees too much. All of these broke Nike's concentration.

By the end of the week, Marta was feeling very discouraged by her slow progress.

"I'm sorry, Nike," she told the mare when they finished for the day. "I just get so scared when you jump. I keep remembering the moment when Tiff made me fall off." She slid off Nike's back and kicked at a browning patch of strawberry clover. She could hear the bovos already in their pens for the day and thought about how hard her family was working to give her this chance to compete in the trials.

Marta sensed Nike knew she had been trying hard. But she still felt like she was letting everyone down.

"I'm afraid," she said in a low voice. "What if I can't do this, Nike? The trials are my only chance to change my family's fortunes. If I fail, we'll be poor forever—and people like the Miltondotters will push us around for the rest of our lives."

As if in reply, Nike sent an image of Marta climbing onto the horse's back. Wondering, Marta slid her leg over the horse's glossy withers and felt her body fall into place. Nike took to the sky, her colorful contrail lighting behind her.

"Where are we going?" Marta asked.

Nike didn't answer. She simply flew on. Before long, they landed at the Grand Monuments at Whitemantle Pass, in Trails End down on the mainland. Marta had always loved the giant rock sculptures of the horses Bella and Bello. More than a thousand years ago, Sigga had asked a sculptor to create the works of art as a tribute to Sara, her adoptive sister and the goddess of all horses in North of North. Sara's horse friend, Bella, was a magnificent white mare and Bello, her mate, was a forceful black stallion.

Once on the ground, Marta dismounted and gazed around, taking in the glorious view. She could spot Rolandsgaard Castle, Sigga's former home, in the distance near Rolands Hold Arena, where the trials would take place. Beyond both the castle and the arena, the sea stretched away to the horizon, glowing in the setting sun.

"This is lovely! Thank you," Marta said to Nike. "But why did you bring me here?"

In her mind, Marta saw an image of an island far out to sea. A fur-clad giant stood by a crumbling stone temple. On the outside of the temple were the words *Have the Courage to Trust Yourself.* Inside the temple a young filly was trapped in a cage with golden bars.

This was the story Mother used to tell me! thought Marta. *This was Nike's story—from Nike's point of view!*

It really happened! Marta realized with wonder. *The stories are true!*

The next image was of the caged filly left all alone on the shore of the island. But then a white light appeared above the water. At the center of the light Marta saw a horse, galloping toward the island over the tops of the waves. *Bella.* A girl in a white frock sat on the horse's back, her golden hair flowing behind her. *That must be Sara,* thought Marta.

As Sara tried to free the filly, the giant appeared, stomping toward them from the ruined temple. The filly neighed, and Sara stepped in front of the cage to shield it from the raging giant. Then Marta gasped as Sara sent a golden thread whirling around the filly. It spun faster and faster until there appeared to be hundreds of strands circling around the horse.

The cage glowed, pulsing red, then yellow, then white. Then the bars vanished. The filly was free—and the giant

was in the cage instead! Marta watched in awe as the young horse unfurled a set of magnificent wings.

I just saw the birth of Nike! Marta thought, and smiled.

As the memory-vision faded, Marta saw that the sun had just dipped beyond the horizon. A cool breeze drifted across the pass. She stroked Nike's arched neck.

"I think I understand why you showed me that memory," she said softly. She realized that she had been feeling trapped—as Nike had been trapped by the cage that bound her. Someone had freed Nike and helped her find her wings when she was a filly, and now Nike was doing the same thing for Marta.

"I'll do it," Marta vowed. "With your help, Nike, I'll break out of my cage and find my own wings!"

The next morning, Marta woke with renewed energy. She and Nike ate their breakfast together at the far end of the clover fields, and then quickly got to work. Marta wanted to practice jumping hedges. Holding onto Nike's mane with just the right amount of pressure, she tried to focus and remember what she needed to do.

Nike began her flying approach toward the hedge. She lifted her legs up high and then beat her wings. At the same time, Marta looked straight ahead, between the horse's ears. This kept her back straight. She and Nike looked like a single unit. As Nike sailed over the hedge, Marta kept her heels down and didn't allow her fear to take over.

Nike cleared the hedge and landed on the other side. They had done it!

"Yes!" Marta yelled. "That was amazing!"

Even a couple of nearby flapuppies whirled their tails in applause.

Nike whinnied happily in agreement. She sent Marta an image of two puzzle pieces that fit together. They were finally a team!

The pair spent the rest of the morning practicing their maneuvers and working on their speed and stamina for the race. Over and over, they practiced picking up objects while in the air, just as they would have to do during the competition.

At the end of the day, Nike soared on the warm thermals, diving in and out of clouds. Marta loved how peaceful it felt to be that high in the sky. Flying with Nike was the most glorious thing she'd ever experienced. She felt so free!

Untying her braided hair, she let the air whip through it. She sat tall and proud on Nike's back and thought, *We may actually have a chance at winning!*

CHAPTER

7

The Festival of Lights finally arrived. On the first day of the celebration, Marta woke especially early to assemble the tubs of strawberry yogurt and butter her mother had left outside. She smiled when she saw the note next to the freshly baked satchel of muffins by the window: *We are so proud of you! Love, Mama, Dad, and Toby.*

Marta carried a pole that went behind her neck and rested across her shoulders. Tubs hung from the pole, making it a heavy burden to carry. Each tub contained jars of yogurt and butter packed in Snowshire Ice, which kept the contents cold for far longer than regular ice. It was useful, but it was heavy!

The sun was making its first appearance as Marta walked to the airship that took her and the other people from her island to Canter Hollow, the village in the heart of Trails End. The sun was barely making its first appearance, but the little town was already bustling in preparation for the festival.

Marta wandered through the twisting streets carrying the heavy tubs. She admired the flowers that were everywhere, splashes of color standing out against the cobblestone streets. Up above, banners hung from every lamppost. On one side, they had an image of an aerial horse flying above Rolands Hold Arena. On the reverse side were the words *Trials of Avensgaard*. Marta brimmed with excitement. This time, *she* was going to be part of the trials!

In the town square, a feeling of nostalgia swept over Marta as she thought of all the times she had run around the horse fountain with her father. Looking around, she saw merchants setting up booths, selling everything from hand-crafted jewelry to decorative pottery to woven linens to food. Wonderful smells filled the air. Marta's stomach growled.

Marta's family couldn't afford to pay for a booth. So like a lot of other people, she was allowed to walk the bustling central square selling her goods. She hoped she could sell all the strawberry yogurt and butter from her bovos. And she needed to do it by noon. That was when all the participants in the Trials of Avensgaard were supposed to be at Rolands Hold Arena to make their entries official.

By midmorning, people flooded Canter Hollow, and the mood was festive. But Marta's feelings were quickly turning to frustration as it became harder and harder for her to push through the crowds with her wares. She felt as if she were getting shoved from every direction. Finally, someone came to her rescue.

"Marta, are you all right?" a voice said.

Marta turned around to see kind Mr. Bartholomew smiling at her from behind his half-moon glasses. Mr. Bartholomew ran a fruit-and-vegetable booth every year. He grew the most incredible plumberries on his farm, and they sold out each year at the festival.

Marta exhaled. "Hi, Mr. Bartholomew. I don't know what to do! I need to sell all of this yogurt and butter, and there are too many people, and I need to get to the arena, and—"

"I can help," the old man interrupted. "Why don't you leave the tubs here? I'll sell them for you and give you the money."

Marta's eyes lit up. "You'd do that for me?"

"Of course," said Mr. Bartholomew. "Now run along."

Marta gave him a grateful smile and unloaded the tubs. "I can't thank you enough," she told him.

Mr. Bartholomew's eyes twinkled. "There *is* one way you can thank me."

"What's that?" asked Marta.

"Win at the trials," Mr. Bartholomew told her. "We're all rooting for you here in town. Just don't let that nasty Miltondotter girl win."

Marta grinned. "I'll do my best!" she promised. "Thanks again. See you soon!"

With her tubs taken care of, Marta made her way to Rolands Hold Arena with a light heart. She remembered hearing that it was Sigga's dream to have a place to hold official equestrian events for thousands of fans. Sigga had placed flags around the horseshoe-shaped arena, and had told the builders to construct an impressive winged horse statue to perch at the top of it. That statue could be seen from the towers at Rolandsgaard Castle.

Marta met Nike just outside the arena, as they had planned. She greeted the horse with an affectionate pat on her flank. Nike whinnied, and the pair went to stand in line.

In the center of the arena, a long table was set up. Behind it sat Mr. Olafsson, the head judge and official in charge of the Trials of Avensgaard. It was his job to meet each horse and rider personally, officially register them, and assign them a color in the race.

There was a wide range of participants. There were girls and boys, mares and stallions, horses and ponies. Marta recognized Britt and Karin, of course, but everyone else was new to her. She had also never before seen such a wide variety of winged horses. There were bright pink ones, pastel blue ones, even a silver-and-white striped one! Marta noticed that many of the horses' tails were braided, some with ribbons woven in.

"That's pretty," Marta said to Nike, pointing them out.

Nike just snorted, as if to say, *Why are you even looking at these lesser beings?*

Marta laughed. "Don't worry. No one is as gorgeous as you are," she said, admiring Nike's own flowing ribbons.

Nike shook out her mane as if in agreement.

Marta noticed that the horse in front of them had wings that were different from Nike's. Looking around, she realized that all the horses had wings as unique as they were. Some had wings that matched the colors and markings of their coats. Others had wings that were one color on the top and another color underneath. Marta was captivated. Remembering Nike's reaction, though, she kept her admiration to herself.

The line seemed to be at a standstill, and Marta peered around the person in front of her to see what the holdup was.

Unsurprisingly, her eyes fell on Tiff Miltondotter, who was waving her hands around as she spoke to Mr. Olafsson. Marta rolled her eyes.

Tiff and her father, Milt Miltondotter, didn't seem to notice the long line behind them. At one point, Marta noticed that Tiff looked over her shoulder and gestured to *her*.

What is she up to? Marta wondered suspiciously.

She soon found out. When she made it to the head of the line and asked to register for the trials, Mr. Olafsson shook his head. "I'm afraid you can't," he informed her.

Marta stared at him blankly. "On what grounds?" she demanded.

"On the grounds that having a common milk maid compete would sully the reputation of the trials," Tiff put in.

"What?" Marta exclaimed.

Mr. Olafsson frowned at Tiff. "Actually, it's because you don't have a Trails End Equestrian Card," he told Marta.

"That's ridiculous!" Marta cried. The Trails End Equestrian Club had been founded by Harald Miltondotter a few years ago. You could belong only if you paid lots of money in dues.

Obviously, Tiff was behind this nonsense because she didn't want Marta in the competition. *This is completely unfair!* Marta thought. She was furious. Tiff didn't need the money. She only wanted to win so she could brag about it.

"I'm sorry, but as Miss Miltondotter points out, it is a requirement. Even though I myself wasn't aware of it until she showed me the rule book," Mr. Olafsson said. He looked very uncomfortable. "It's new."

Nike snorted and reared back, spreading her wings. They were so white, they glowed. Her ribbons billowed out behind her, and her eyes shone more brilliantly than Marta had ever seen. The entire arena fell silent. Everyone stared at the spectacular mare.

Mr. Olafsson's mouth opened and closed. He could hardly put words together. "Oh . . . Oh, my! . . . How magnificent!"

Then Nike projected an image into both Marta's and Mr. Olafsson's heads. It showed the trials, hundreds of years earlier, when Sigga herself was the head judge. As horses and riders approached, she asked only their names. From the look of the ragged clothes of some of the participants, it was clear that the trials were open to anyone, not just the wealthy.

Mr. Olafsson dropped his head in shame. Then he looked up again, with a glint in his eyes. "I shall take the rule book to the judges' panel for review and correction after the trials are over. In the meantime, I shall allow Marta Thomas and Nike to enter."

Marta's smile stretched from ear to ear. "Thank you," she whispered to Nike.

"This is outrageous!" Tiff whined, stomping on the ground like a little girl. "Do something, Daddy!"

But even Mr. Miltondotter seemed impressed by Nike.

Marta walked right up to Tiff. "That'll teach you to mess with a Thomas," she said in a voice that only Tiff could hear.

Then Marta and Nike walked out of the arena, a newfound lightness in their steps.

That evening, Marta stood next to Nike as the fireworks show began. Musicians played as one firecracker after another was sent into the night sky. The rockets jetted across the sky, exploding in colorful displays. Fireworks that suddenly changed into galloping horses or fire-breathing dragons amazed and enchanted the crowds below.

Marta found herself thinking of times past. Her father had always brought her to the Festival of Lights. It was their special time together, and Marta looked forward to it all year. They would feast on their favorite festival treat, cobs of corn slathered with melted butter. Every year, too, Marta would beg her father to buy her a flowered garland with long ribbons to wear on her head. He always said yes, even though the garland would only last for one day and then the petals would begin to fall off.

The previous year, she had not wanted a garland. "They're for children, and I'm not a little girl anymore," she'd told her father. Her dad had looked strangely heartbroken. Thinking of it now, Marta felt a lump in her throat. She'd barely seen her parents all day, but suddenly she wished they were with her so she could curl up and put her head in Mama's lap.

Then a red-and-white firework lit up the sky like an illuminated candy cane. Nike whinnied and Marta was caught up in the excitement again.

Although the sparkling lights and celebrations continued late into the night, Marta left early. She had a big day ahead of her and wanted to be well rested for the tournament.

Once at home, though, she could hardly sleep. The anticipation of the next day's events kept her awake for hours. *I can't believe this is actually happening to me*, she thought, hugging her Nike-patterned quilt to her. She smiled and turned on her side, warm with the promise of good things to come.

She and Nike had practiced. They had rehearsed the rings and obstacles. They had trained hard for the race. Now there was only one thing left to do.

Win!

Near the Rolands Hold Arena, a shadow appeared, visible only by the light of the fireworks overhead. The figure fumbled with a set of keys and then opened the door to the warehouse where the magical rings and obstacles were stored. The mysterious figure went inside.

A few minutes later, the figure emerged from the warehouse, looking around quickly to make sure no one else was there. The sky erupted in a cascading firework, momentarily lighting up the shadowed face.

It was Tiff Miltondotter.

8

The next morning, with much fanfare, the Trials of Avensgaard began. Rolands Hold Arena was filled with excited, screaming fans. Marta, Nike, and the other competitors waited in a holding area and watched as a grand procession of flags, representing all the participants, marched through the arena. Following that were musicians wearing velvet robes and hats and playing long, brass trumpets.

Mr. Olafsson and the other two judges made their appearances next and walked up a flight of stairs to a balcony where they would view and score the maneuvers. Mr. Olafsson waved to the crowd as he walked, but he did not get the applause he usually received each year. Word had spread about his initial refusal to let Marta and Nike enter the tournament. That didn't make him the most popular man.

A change of music signified that it was time for the riders and their horses to make their entrances. The horses walked in a single file line, the riders astride them, waving to the crowd as they made their way into the arena. Each pair wore a specific color—the riders on their jackets and hats, the horses on their ribbons. The color matched the color of the objects each team needed to gather during the race.

Tiff and Alrek trotted into the arena dressed in cardinal red. Tiff's jacket looked sharp and crisp against her blond hair, and Alrek was adorned with multiple crimson ribbons. Behind them, Britt and Roald arrived in gold, and Karin and Dagna wore sapphire blue. When Marta and Nike appeared in varying shades of purple, the crowd erupted into cheers.

It did seem as if the whole town were rooting for them. *Maybe Mr. Bartholomew wasn't kidding!* Marta thought gleefully. She felt an extra boost of confidence from the warm reception.

All the participants took a lap around the arena. Tiff and Alrek insisted on being in front and practically pushed their way to get there. On the second lap, the horses took to the air, to the great delight of the crowd. With all the different-colored contrails, the sky became a rainbow of color.

After the opening ceremonies were complete, the participants were ushered back into the holding area. The first event was the rings, followed by the obstacle course. Six magical rings floated in the sky, and the competitors needed to fly through the center of each ring without touching the edges. The trick was that the rings expanded or contracted at odd intervals, so you had to time it just right.

The twelve competitors had drawn numbers to set the order. Marta and Nike were first.

"Ready, Nike?" Marta said, as she mounted the winged horse. Her stomach fluttered. Rings and obstacles had been their best event in practice, but she was still very nervous.

The horse whinnied loudly and took to the sky with a flourish, her massive wings spread wide. They flew over the cheering crowd in the stands below and climbed high toward the first ring.

One after another, Marta and Nike flew through the rings. Nike's grace and control enabled her to bring her wings into her body at just the right moment. Their timing and execution was perfect, and they earned full points.

Then it was time for obstacles. Marta and Nike easily flew over a hedge, a fence, and an oxer—a type of jump with two poles at unequal heights. As Nike nailed jump after jump, Marta began to relax. So far, they had a perfect score! There was only one obstacle left: a triple bar. You needed to go under and over the bars, rather than just soar over the top one, as you would on the ground. It was tricky, but Marta and Nike had pulled it off perfectly the last few times they'd practiced.

Nike flew toward the triple bar, her wings flapping in a steady rhythm. Marta kept her head up and her gaze forward. Nike flew over the first pole and then immediately dipped under the next one. But on the third and final one, the pole suddenly floated away!

Marta was stunned. She was certain neither she nor Nike had done anything to cause the pole to dislodge or break away. She could hear that the audience, too, was astounded. They gasped and pointed from the stands.

The judges took a few minutes to discuss the matter. They flew up to inspect the jump, but could find nothing wrong with it. Finally, they announced their decision: A point would be deducted from Marta and Nike's score.

Marta was frustrated. Nike hadn't touched the pole—it must have had something wrong with it! She felt they should get another chance. But no matter how much she protested, it made no difference. The judges' decision was final.

The crowd booed. Marta and Nike hung their heads low, feeling very disappointed as they headed toward the holding area.

"That was so strange," Tiff commented as they passed by. "I've never seen a pole break away like that. I wonder if perhaps it wasn't set up correctly," she added innocently.

Marta stopped in her tracks. She'd just had a terrible thought. "Tiff, did you have something to do with it?"

Tiff gasped dramatically. "Me? Of course not! I would never do such a thing!" she said. Then she gave a nasty smile and whispered, "And anyway, you'd never prove it."

Marta's eyes blazed. She'd never felt so angry! She felt completely certain that Tiff had sabotaged her and Nike. But equally, she had no idea how to prove it.

Nike snorted and pranced, eyeing Alrek with a hostile glare. Marta felt a little better when she saw that Tiff's big stallion was cowed. But only a little.

With the pole of the triple bar now back in place and secured, Britt and Roald were next. They flew up above the arena and began their maneuvers. They tackled the rings first and did well, getting only a minor deduction for Roald's wings hitting the side of a spinning ring. They completed the obstacles without any trouble, although they lost a point for presentation because Britt's face was so sullen the whole time she performed.

Following Britt was Malachi, a boy from Clonia. He wore long, flowing garments and rode a gorgeous stallion named Gypsy. As the pair soared up to the rings, the arena was alive with girls gossiping about the handsome bronze-skinned boy.

But Malachi kept his focus on the competition. He and Gypsy performed well, although Gypsy hesitated before a floating hedge, so points were deducted. The girls in the audience still gave them an ecstatic round of applause.

Next, it was Karin and Dagna's turn. Karin was a natural at riding and performing, and she and Dagna performed quite well. They were a little shaky on the contracting and expanding rings, but it was mostly because of bad luck. Dagna spooked, startled when a bird flew through one of the rings just as she approached it. On the second try, though, Karin and Dagna successfully flew through the ring.

After all the others, it was finally Tiff Miltondotter's turn. She and Alrek gave a flawless performance. They completed the rings with ease and coasted over and under the obstacles with never a false move. When they landed, Tiff smiled broadly. She dismounted Alrek, gave a wave to the crowd, and then walked back to the holding area.

"*That's* how it's done," she said to Marta smugly.

Marta just ignored her. She'd had enough of Tiff to last her a lifetime.

There were two more events that day. Late that afternoon the competitors gathered to see the final standings. Only the top five scorers from that day would be eligible to compete in the race the following day.

Marta had been keeping close track of the scores all day, so there were no surprises. Nevertheless, she was thrilled when the judges announced the results.

Tiff and Alrek were in the lead,

with Marta and Nike right behind them—trailing by only one point. Following them were Karin and Dagna, Malachi and Gypsy, and in fifth place, Britt and Roald.

Marta was bursting with happiness. "We did it, Nike," she whispered, as she hugged the horse, brushing her cheek against Nike's soft mane.

Tiff sneered. "You got lucky," she told Marta. "You don't stand a chance tomorrow."

Marta simply smiled. She couldn't wait to prove Tiff wrong.

Day two of the Trials of Avensgaard began bright and early.
Marta had hardly slept the night before.
She was up even before the first bovo
mooed. She tried to keep her nerves
under control as she thought about
today's long, difficult race.

It was a scavenger hunt. Everyone had the same list of objects they had
to gather along the way, but you had to
make sure to collect the ones that were
in your color. The team that gathered all
the objects of their assigned color and

crossed the finish line first would win.

As Marta and Nike made their way to Rolands Hold Arena, Marta saw fans and spectators lined up along the route to cheer on the race teams. Many had arrived early to assure a good viewing spot.

At the arena, the five riders groomed their horses and studied the map of the course. The horses were once again adorned with flowing ribbons, each matching its rider's assigned color. Marta and the other riders put on their competition outfits and gear. Then it was time for the riders and their horses to line up side by side.

At exactly nine o'clock a green flag was waved—and the race began!

Marta and Nike took to the air along with the others. All five of the horses were fast flyers, although Marta was sure Nike could beat them all in a straight race. The key with this race was retrieving your objects without slowing down.

The first destination was the Bella and Bello monuments. Each team had to grab a floating ribbon as they flew between the monuments. All the ribbons were at different heights so no one would collide. Nike and Marta easily retrieved their purple ribbon. As far as Marta could tell, no one else had any trouble with that task, either.

Then they looped around to head toward Horseshoe Bay, where Starguide Lighthouse stood. Sailors and horses used the lighthouse's shining ruby as a beacon to show them the way to Trails End. For the race, Marta and the other participants needed to grab a floating star that hovered around the face of the lighthouse. Timing was essential, for the bright ruby light was not something you'd want to look directly into. If you got caught in the full force of the tremendous light, it could temporarily blind you.

Britt and Roald made it to Starguide Lighthouse first, but Britt missed their yellow star on their first approach. They had to circle back around, losing valuable time as they waited for the lighthouse light to revolve once more.

Tiff and Alrek had seen Britt's mistake. Tiff made sure she didn't make the same one. She expertly grasped her red star on her first attempt.

Right behind her were Marta and Nike.

"A little bit closer," Marta urged. The glowing purple star was almost in her reach.

Nike gave a delicate flutter of her wings, and Marta snatched the floating star. "Got it!" she declared triumphantly.

A great cheer rose up. The fans on the ground and inside the lighthouse clapped wildly as Marta and Nike flew away. Marta felt a flush of warmth in her heart. The poor girl from the Overgaard Skylands was still the crowd favorite!

The competitors flew on to Rolandsgaard Castle. Tiff was in the lead, with Marta, Karin, and Malachi close behind. Britt and Roald were still trying to catch up. Each team needed to pick up a flag from one of the castle turrets.

Out of the corner of her eye, Marta saw a blur of red and black coming toward Karin and Dagna. *Whoosh!* It zoomed right in front of them, making Dagna backpedal in midair. Karin jerked back in her seat, and Marta could see Karin's mouth drop open in surprise as she stared at Tiff and Alrek.

"Oh, sorry," Tiff said, acting innocent.

Both Marta and Karin knew that nothing Tiff did was by accident. Tiff wanted to win the race, but Marta hadn't guessed that Tiff would sabotage even her own friend.

Marta saw Karin's eyes narrow in anger as she flew back up to grab her blue flag from the castle turret.

"Wow, Nike. Tiff will stop at nothing

to get what she wants, will she?" Marta murmured, as they flew over a thermal airstream.

Nike shuddered.

"My thoughts exactly!" Marta agreed, shaking her head.

Legendary Drasilmare, the great tree, was the next destination. Alrek and Nike were neck and neck as they flew into the branches of the gigantic tree. The goal was to retrieve a specific flower—without disturbing a single leaf in the process. It required great control and skill on the horses' parts because of their massive wings.

Tiff and Marta plucked their flowers as their horses expertly maneuvered between the leaves of the great tree. Behind them, as Malachi scooped up his orange flower, Gypsy narrowly missed colliding with a giant branch.

"Yes!" the boy called. The three of them flew out of the tree just as Karin and Britt and their horses flew in.

"We've already got four of our race items," Marta said excitedly to Nike. "Only two more to go!"

Nike sent an image of the next object: a purple orb. Marta understood that the mare wanted her to stay focused. The pair headed toward the waterfall.

The waters of Teardrop Falls began at the edge of a lake near Drasilmare. In a tremendous rush, the water cascaded into a series of falls that ended in a roaring cloud of mist. An undeniable magic infused the falls. At times, the water seemed to be falling up instead of down, or even frozen in time. The citizens of Trails End knew they needed to be careful near the falls. Although the falls were impressive, they were also very treacherous.

For this part of the race, as each team approached the falls, a colored orb would pitch itself into the dangerous waters below. The horse and rider would need to fly down and retrieve their object before it—and they—plunged into the raging rapids. Marta had heard stories of the many competitors who were unable to complete this difficult part of the race because of the constantly changing speed and direction of the falls. It often caused the horses to become disoriented.

It didn't seem to be a problem for Tiff and Alrek as the pair successfully recovered their red orb.

"Nice, Alrek!" Tiff said proudly, as Alrek pulled up out of the dive.

Alrek whinnied triumphantly in response.

Malachi and Gypsy were not as lucky. As they approached the falls, Gypsy began to spook. No matter how many times Malachi tried to reassure his horse that it was all right, Gypsy wouldn't fly over the falls. To his and the crowd's disappointment, Malachi was forced to withdraw from the race.

The crowd cheered as Marta and Nike approached. A purple orb began its descent down the falls. Marta leaned forward, gripping tightly with her knees. She and Nike streamlined their position for maximum speed. The orb plummeted down, and Nike raced after it.

"Yes, Nike!" Marta exclaimed, as the falls froze into a solid, glassy wall of ice.

Just as Marta snatched the orb out of the air, something caught her eye. In a thick briar patch at the falls' edge, she saw something that looked strangely familiar.

Her eyes widened as she took a closer look. With one black ear and one white ear, there was no mistaking it: It was the bovo that had wandered away from her family farm all those weeks ago!

The falls instantly turned from ice back into rushing water again. The noise pounded in Marta's ears. Her thoughts whirled. *How had the bovo gotten here?*

Nike whinnied. "You're right," Marta said. "Let's go!" Now was not the time to figure it out. They could return for the animal after the race ended.

Suddenly, a shriek echoed in her ears. Marta turned to see a roc circling high in the sky. The giant bird of prey was known for its keen eyesight. There was no way it would fail to notice the trapped bovo.

Marta had only a split second to make a decision: finish the race or save the bovo. It was clear to her, though, what her choice had to be.

"Nike!" Marta shouted, squashing down her disappointment. "The bovo! She's in trouble! We've got to save her."

Immediately, Nike swooped up and out of the rushing water. Marta desperately looked for a familiar face among the spectators lined up along the rocky edge of the falls. Then she spotted Malachi.

"Let's get Malachi to help," Marta suggested. At the top of the falls, Nike dived down and Marta swiftly grabbed the boy's wrist, hoisting him onto Nike's back.

Malachi looked surprised, but Marta quickly explained the predicament. "We haven't got much time," she told him.

Nike's speed brought the group to the bovo in seconds. The bovo was lowing softly in pain. Marta could see why: The plants of the briar patch were digging into its skin. Nike stood guard as Marta and Malachi worked furiously to free the trapped animal.

Nike whinnied urgently, and when Marta looked over her shoulder, she saw that the roc had begun its dive. "Hurry!" she cried.

The roc shrieked as it swooped down toward its prey.

With only seconds to spare, the bovo was finally free. Malachi quickly led it into a cave where they'd be safe. They made it just in time! The roc swooped down, but it couldn't fit inside the small cave opening. It squawked loudly with rage.

Marta remounted Nike. Looking up, she was thrilled to see people already making their way down the rocky path to help. She called out to

Malachi, "Help is on the way!"

"Don't worry about us," called Malachi. "Go and finish the race!"

Finish the race? Marta didn't think they stood a chance of winning.

Instantly, an image of the golden horseshoes filled Marta's head. Nike wanted to finish the race, whether or not they had a chance to win! Then Nike sent an image of a first-place medal around Marta's neck, followed by an image of a second-place medal around Tiff's neck.

Marta giggled. "I'd like to see Tiff come in second, too," she told Nike. "Okay, let's see if we can make up the time we lost. If anyone can do it, you can, Nike."

Exhilaration rushed through Marta as she and Nike flew across Naastrand Sound to begin the flight up Mt. White-mantle.

Marta had thought their bovo detour put them out of the race. But she hadn't reckoned with Nike's astounding speed in the air. Her massive wings ate up the distance faster than Marta had believed possible. They outpaced the wind. Marta's hair whipped straight back and tears streamed from her eyes as they tore up the mountainside.

Near the peak, they passed Britt and Roald, who were having a tough time with the almost-vertical faces of the highest mountain in North of North. There were no thermals to soar on here, no place to coast or stop and rest your wings. Roald was simply worn out.

Seconds later, Marta and Nike passed Karin and Dagna, who were also struggling.

Now the peak was in sight. Marta let out a cry of disappointment as she spotted Tiff and Alrek, who had already landed. As Marta watched, Tiff leaned down from Alrek's back and plucked a red crystal from a rock formation.

"We might be able to beat them on the way back down," Marta said to Nike.

Nike's chest was heaving with exhaustion from her sprint, but she tossed her head and snorted as if to say, *No doubt!*

Nike glided in to land as Tiff and Alrek took off. Nearby, Marta spotted a gold crystal, a blue crystal, and an orange one, tucked into niches in the jagged rocks. But where was the purple? She couldn't see it anywhere. Dismounting, she began to hunt around.

From up above, Tiff's nasty laugh floated down faintly. Something made Marta lift her eyes to the sky.

She gasped as she saw a flash of purple in Tiff's hand. Tiff had stolen her crystal!

A second later Tiff opened her hand and let the purple crystal fall. It tumbled through the air, sparkling in the sunlight, turning end over end— straight toward a deep, narrow crevice in the mountain.

"No!" The cry tore from Marta's throat.

There were no judges up there, no fans. No one to witness Tiff brazenly cheating.

Marta stood there, aghast. Just like that, Tiff had stolen not just the race, but Marta's chance to change her family's fortunes! How could she be so cruel?

Then a blue, brown, and white blur shot past on Marta's left. Karin and Dagna! They raced not for the blue crystal, but for the purple one that was falling through the air. With a mighty effort, Karin caught the crystal in her outstretched hand just before it vanished into the crevice.

Marta gaped in sheer astonishment.

Karin and Dagna circled around and flew back toward Marta. Karin dropped the purple crystal at Marta's feet. "Better get going," she said with a smile.

"Karin! What do you think you're doing?!" Tiff yelled.

"Playing fair, for a change," Karin called back. "You should try it sometime."

As Marta mounted Nike, Tiff screeched with fury. "Karin, you traitor!"

Her cry was so loud that Alrek spooked and reared.

"*Ahhh!*" Tiff shrieked, grabbing his mane as she lost her balance.

With a tinkling sound, all of her race objects slid out of her bag—and plummeted into the same crevice where Marta's crystal had almost disappeared forever.

Nike let out a whinny that sounded like laughter. Karin and Marta looked at each other and grinned. Then Karin plucked her blue crystal. "Race you to the bottom," she said to Marta.

"You're on!" Marta agreed happily. "Oh—and by the way, thank you!"

As they took off on Nike and Dagna, Tiff stared after them, red-faced with rage. The race was over for her and Alrek.

As they shot down the mountain, Nike and Dagna were neck and neck. Dagna was a bigger horse, which gave him a wider wingspan. But Nike had more power. First, one pulled ahead, and then the other. But neither could establish a clear lead.

Marta laughed aloud with joy. This was the way the race should have been all along!

"There they are!" someone shouted as the horses drew near the arena. The entire crowd began to roar with excitement. Nike and Dagna flew across the sky, their contrails overlapping in a sparkling display.

And then they were hurtling toward the black-and-white floating marker in front of the judges' balcony. That was the finish line.

"Go, Nike," Marta whispered.

Nike's ears flicked back as she heard

the soft plea. Her muscles bunched under Marta's hands, and then she poured all her power into one great wing-thrust.

Phoom! Nike and Dagna shot across the finish line together. But one horse was ahead by a proud nose.

Nike!

The thunderous applause that erupted in the arena over-whelmed Marta. She tried to take it all in. She couldn't believe the crowd was cheering for *them*. She still couldn't believe they had actually won.

Nike absolutely basked in the glory. She loved this kind of attention! Marta giggled as Nike preened and posed, open-ing her wings and rearing on her hind legs to elicit wild cheers from the fans. Then the pair flew a victory lap around the arena, diving down and soaring sky high, much to the delight of the enthusiastic crowd.

It wasn't until the second lap that it sank in that this wasn't a dream. It really had happened!

"We did it, Nike!" Marta cried happily. "We really did it!"

Nike did a final loop in the air and then landed in the center of the arena.

"Congratulations! Congratulations!" exclaimed Mr. Olafsson, rushing over. "A magnificent race! The most spectacular finish I've ever seen!"

As Mr. Olafsson went to congratulate Karin and Dagna, Marta turned to say something to Nike.

Nike was gone! Marta looked all around, but saw no sign of her.

She wouldn't leave before we got our prize, would she? Marta wondered uneasily.

"Come, come!" Mr. Olafsson said, as he ushered Marta over to the winner's circle for the awards ceremony. "Where is your horse friend?"

"Um, I'm sure she'll be back in a moment," Marta said, hoping she was right.

She took her place in the center. Next to her stood Karin and Dagna. In third place were Britt and Roald, who had crossed the finish line while Nike and Marta were on their victory lap.

"Congratulations," Karin told Marta.

"Thanks," Marta replied. "It was a close race."

"Yes, but you won it, fair and square," replied Karin. She sounded like she meant it.

Marta cleared her throat. "I want to thank you for what you did on the mountain."

"You're welcome," said Karin. "Tiff needs some lessons in good horsemanship."

Marta giggled.

Just then Nike flew back into the arena. Marta's heart lifted. And lifted still more as she saw the passengers Nike carried on her back. Marta's family! Mama sat behind Marta's father, Toby cradled in her arms. Nike landed, and some of the townspeople reached up to help the injured Mr. Thomas climb down.

Marta ran over and hugged them tightly.

"Oh, Marta, love," said Mrs. Thomas, tears glistening in her eyes. "We are so very proud of you."

Mr. Thomas lifted Marta's chin. "My brave girl," he said. "You did it."

Marta beamed. She *had* done it.

Mr. Olafsson cleared his throat. "Marta, if you wouldn't mind—"

"Yes, yes, I'm coming!" Marta said quickly. She ran back to the winner's circle, but not before giving each of her parents—and Toby—a kiss on the cheek. Then Nike accompanied Marta to her place of honor.

"Thank you, Nike," she whispered. "Thank you for bringing my family here."

With a fanfare of trumpets and the ecstatic crowd on its feet, the awards ceremony began. Karin and Britt and their horses received medals for placing second and third. The girls smiled and waved to the audience and their families.

Then Mr. Olafsson stepped in front of Marta and Nike. "And to Marta Thomas, the winner of this year's Trials of Avensgaard, I present this solid gold medal—and these golden horseshoes." He stepped back and waved at a cart that had just been towed in by six uniformed guards. It was heaped high with glittering golden shoes.

Marta gasped. Her parents gasped. The entire crowd gasped. That was a lot of horseshoes!

"Thank you, Mr. Olafsson," Marta managed. Still in shock, she bent her head to receive the medal around her neck. "Thank you, everyone!" she shouted at the enthusiastic crowd. Then, turning to Nike, she threw her arms around the

chestnut mare's neck. "And especially you, Nike," she whispered. "None of it would be possible without you."

Nike whinnied cheerfully, her eyes sparkling like diamonds. Then with her nose, she nudged Marta forward to soak up the glory that she had earned. Marta waved at the crowd and felt happier than she ever had in her life.

And she knew just what she was going to do with the golden horseshoes.

The next morning, a gentle whinny woke Marta up. Throwing her quilt over her shoulders, she stepped outside.

"Nike," said Marta quietly. She patted the horse's velvety nose. A tear rolled down her cheek. Without knowing *how* she knew, she sensed that it was time for Nike to leave.

"I'm going to miss you so much!" she said.

Nike nuzzled Marta's arm and blew softly through her nostrils.

Marta began to sob. She hugged Nike tightly, feeling the mare's soft mane against her neck.

A pictured formed in Marta's head: the wagonload of golden horseshoes.

That was a cheerful thought! Marta wiped away her tears. "You know what I'm going to do with them?" she asked the horse.

Nike shook her head.

"I'm going to buy this entire island!" Marta said, her eyes dancing with excitement. "I worked it out with Mama and Dad last night. Even if Mr. Miltondotter charges us top price, we'll still have enough left to hire some farm workers to help out. And I just might have some left over to build a stable for a flying horse," she added a little shyly.

Nike drew back and snorted. It was perfectly clear that she was offended.

"What are you mad about?" Marta chided. "I'm talking about *you*, silly. Who did you think I meant?" Then she grew serious. "You know that if you ever need a home, you'll have one here with me."

Nike whinnied appreciatively. Then she stretched her wings wide and took to the sky. Marta watched in awe as the magnificent mare soared away, her contrail glimmering in the rising sun.

iona was even more beautiful than Astrid could have imagined. Tall, sleek, and regal, the stunning mare had a fiery red coat and a mane that fell nearly to her knees.

"This is Astrid," Philenia told the mare. "She needs to get home. Can you help?"

The horse bowed her shapely head and gazed at Astrid with her dark, liquid eyes. In her mind, Astrid felt the mare's assent and gasped aloud with wonder.

"She—I heard her—I mean, I felt her—" Astrid babbled in amazement.

Then she swallowed hard, trying to regain control of her senses so as not to appear foolish. That was what horses did, after all—they sent their thoughts and emotions directly to the person with whom they wished to communicate. True, none of the horses Astrid knew had ever bothered to communicate with her in that way. Her grandfather's horse Paal had always managed to make his feelings known through more ordinary means.

Is it always so special? Astrid wondered. *Or does it feel this way because it's Fiona?*

"Come, my dear," Philenia said to Astrid. "It is dark, and your family will be worried. You had better get going."

Astrid felt a little shy about mounting the glorious mare. However, Fiona had already stepped over to stand beside one of the boulders. Before she knew it, Astrid felt her body settling into place as if she'd ridden Fiona many times before.

"Thank you," Astrid said. "Thank you so much. It was wonderful to meet you."

Philenia smiled. "Likewise, my dear," she said. "Now enjoy the trip home—and hang on!

Before Astrid could wonder how Philenia knew about Paal, she felt the great red horse's muscles gather beneath her. She gasped at the feeling of power in the mare's hindquarters as she sprang into a smooth, effortless trot. Fiona was moving faster than Astrid had ever gone before—faster than she'd believed possible. It was still raining, but somehow the horse seemed to dodge between the raindrops, and Astrid remained dry.

Despite such speed, Astrid found the mare's stride smooth and easy. It was so smooth, in fact, that she couldn't help noticing an occasional bobble, the tiniest hesitation in Fiona's stride. What could it mean? Then she forgot about that as Fiona once again began sending images into her mind. She saw four yearlings frolicking on the shores of Teardrop Lake—a glowing red filly, a doe-eyed flaxen chestnut with a tiny set of wings, a sturdy black colt with a lightning-shaped mark across his hindquarters, and a slender-legged bay filly with a pretty, delicately chiseled face. The four young horses grazed and played, carefree and happy.

The red filly lifted her head from the grass as a child came into view—a girl, innocent and sweet yet somehow sad. After that, each image came quickly and fluttered away again, like scattering butterflies. A regal white mare. A lotus flower upon the still water. A woman sitting at a loom weaving an intricate tapestry . . .

Astrid's eyes flew open. She stared into the darkness without seeing. She had heard countless stories of the first meeting of the four most renowned horses in North of North. It was said to have taken place at the gathering held many, many years ago to celebrate the hundredth anniversary of the forming of the Valkyrie Sisterhood.

According to the legends, that girl in the images was Sara, the child goddess. The other three yearlings were Nike, Thunder, and Jewel. And the fourth young horse was Fiona herself.

The knowledge that she had been given the gift of meeting the now-grown Fiona, of riding her just as she'd imagined so many times, was so overwhelming that Astrid's eyes filled with tears of joy.

Go to
www.bellasara.com
and enter the webcode below.
Enjoy!

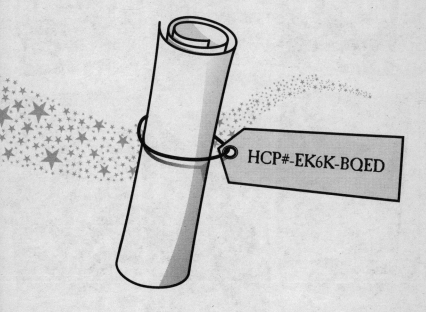

HCP#-EK6K-BQED